Homecoming

A novella by
Tanya Bullock

blackbird

First published in 2016 by

Blackbird Digital Books
2/25 Earls Terrace
London W8 6LP

www.blackbird-books.com

A CIP catalogue record for this book is available from the British Library

ISBN: 978-0-993307-06-5

Cover design by Darren Lewis

WHAT ADVANCE READERS ARE SAYING

'A beautiful love story. Quite simply stunning and poetic.' — Adele, Goodreads librarian

'Definitely the strangest love story I have ever read. Read in one sitting.' — Nats, Goodreads

'*Homecoming* is unique which is truly difficult to find in modern fiction. For originality, excellent character development and for living up to the hype, I rate this novella as 5 out of 5 stars.' — Amie Gaudet, Amie's Book Reviews, Top #50 Canadian Goodreads reviewer

'Just read the book until it reaches your heart ... every page you turn, there is something new but very unusual.' — Laura Prime, Goodreads

'A novella that falls far from the mainstream love stories we find ourselves consuming these days. Being someone who truly appreciates beautiful writing, it wasn't hard for me to complete this book in one sitting.' — Nihaad Gamieldien, Read and Seek

'This author has a real gift for word craft. Homecoming is a uniquely told love story ... a lovely, lovely read.' — T.S Harvey, Author

'I loved it.' — Sarah, By The Letter Book Reviews

'A wonderful surprise; a twist on a well-loved genre that will delight and tug at the heart strings. One of the most touching romantic tales I've read in a long time.' — Shelley Wilson, Author

'Love weaves through it in colourful strands, radiating out from the funny, plucky heroine to those around her ... A beautiful and satisfying read.' — Sandra Peachey, Peachey Letters Blog

'This is the type of story that makes you feel a certain way after you read it. For me, it was a bittersweet longing ... a lovely story told in an interesting way.' — Kerrie Irish, Chat About Books

For Katia and Jake

Chapter One

Rosie loved Tom. Rosie had *always* loved Tom and, although she was unable to measure "always" in terms of years and months, this made perfect sense to her. Their love was not constrained by the mortal bonds of time; it was eternal, ageless and ancient beyond all recollection and record. All that mattered to Rosie, all that had ever really mattered, was that she loved him and he loved her. These facts, she knew, were as solid and undeniable as the old oak tree in the garden. Nowadays, Tom talked to the oak tree more than he did to Rosie, but she didn't take this personally. She understood his need to be with nature. She knew he found it comforting that a world which produced guns and bombs could also yield a dewy spring blossom. She realised that his eyes craved beauty, for she had only to look into them to see that his wounds were still fresh and current. He needed time, she told herself. He hadn't long come home and it was clearly going to take a little while longer for him to truly return to her. It didn't make the slightest difference to how she felt about him. She had all the time in the world for Tom and, while she waited for him, their love would see them through.

Tom found the sudden change in his circumstances more than a little bewildering. To be here in the house, shadowed by his watchful, yet unobtrusive wife was wonderful, but also rather strange. It felt like the fantasies he'd created as a battle-weary soldier, when he'd shunned grim reality in favour of a romanticised vision of life back in England. He'd so often dreamed of home, that his homecoming had seemed dreamlike and still now his surroundings quivered with the tremulous contours of a mirage. Yet, for all its perplexing intensity, Tom was acutely aware that life here was good. The house was beautiful and so was she. It was his favourite time of year; the garden was brimming with burgeoning flowers, the house was bathed in the mellow luminosity of hazy spring sunshine and his wife… his wife's blue eyes shimmered with the promise of better times to come. It was the culmination of his most cherished desires. His home, his garden and his lovely wife, waiting for him at the end of it all. Tom knew he would be happy, given time.

Rosie noticed that the ritual of familiar routine helped Tom adjust to his new environment. He took to making the bed with her, helping her set the table, putting out his West Ham mug next to her china teacup as she filled the kettle. The more time Tom spent at home with Rosie, the more ownership he took of his daily chores and, much to her satisfaction, he even began to instigate them. One Sunday morning, she found him in the kitchen, peeling potatoes and carrots for lunch. She watched him for a few moments, mesmerised by the rhythmic motion of his task and by the perfectly proportioned strips of orange vegetable peel emanating from the carrot in his hand. She bustled into the room.

'You don't need a housewife,' she joked.

He put down the carrot and took her in his arms.

'But I'll always need a wife,' he replied.

Rosie thrilled at his words and at his touch. After so long apart, his skin on hers felt like the very first time. She cast her mind back to that exquisite night, not so very long ago, when their future together had stretched out before them, as long and as vibrant as their tightly intertwined limbs. She wished now she'd made a note of that date; the day they realised the full extent of their feelings for each other, the day that changed both their lives forever. Why is it, she thought to herself, that I can remember every look, every smell, every *taste* from that night, but I don't know whether it was July or January? She put it down to the heady excitement of first love and, as she looked into Tom's eyes now, she knew he could still make her feel that way.

A few days later, he kissed her full on the lips, catching her unawares while she took tea in the garden. The shock of it caused her to drop her favourite cup and, as she responded to the warm pressure of his mouth, she watched the shards of rose-patterned porcelain scatter across the veranda. She tried to focus on his kiss, the sweetness of which she had sorely missed, but her mind returned to the shattered pieces of bone china surrounding them. She fancied they were like splinters of fractured time; fragmented moments from their past together. Time they had wasted, time they had borrowed, time they had taken for granted and would never get back.

That night they lay down together, face-to-face on one pillow. Rosie held her breath and listened to the sounds of the silence; the dripping tap, the ticking clock, Tom's steady breathing. She looked deep into the whirlpool of his cloudy gaze, trying to interpret its meaning and feeling much like Alice tumbling down the rabbit-hole; dizzy with excitement, yet fearful she would lose herself in the sensation of perpetual falling.

'I love you, Tom,' she croaked.

He shifted beside her.

'I should go back to my own bed.'

She squeezed her eyelids shut and tried hard to understand.

'This is your bed too,' she told him, 'whenever you're ready.'

He stroked her face and kissed her affectionately on the forehead.

'Good-night, my love.'

He rose from the bed and left her staring into the shadows. She lay awake for a while, doggedly counting her blessings; but then the creeping darkness slowly dimmed her senses and sleep erased her memory until all that remained in her consciousness was the imprint of her sorrow.

Tom lay trembling in an unfamiliar bed across the landing. He thought about his wife, about her sparkling sea-blue eyes. She was all he'd ever wanted in a woman. Why then, when he loved her so much, when his body *ached* for her, was he spending the night alone, yet again? He was tired, that he knew and he'd been through so much, but coming home to her had helped soothe the pain and he was now ready to put the past behind him. Tomorrow he would talk to her, explain how he really felt. He'd get a few things off his chest, about the loneliness and the fear. Clear the air so to speak. She'd understand. He needed to talk, to get back to his old self and then they could get on with the business of living.

The next morning, Tom found her in the garden, barefoot and dressed only in a thin dressing-gown. She didn't notice him at first, so enthralled was she by the dancing daffodils under the oak tree, by the sweet birdsong and the long wet grass, which felt like tiny puppy tongues lapping her ankles.

'You'll catch your death, you silly old moo,' he reproached her mildly.

She turned to him laughing and shivering, delighted that he'd sought her out.

'Watch it, cheeky!' she said. 'I'm not old.'

'Well you're too old to be wandering around outside half-clothed,' he grumbled as he guided her gently back into the house.

'I was going to have a bath,' she told him, 'but I looked out the window and the garden looked so pretty.'

They sat down in the living room together and she put her hands in his.

'Do you remember when we used to do silly things? Just for the fun of it?'

He shook his head.

'No, not really. Can't say I do.'

She leant forward and searched his eyes.

'Of *course* you do,' she insisted. 'Running down hills, blowing spit bubbles. Skinny-dipping.'

She wiggled her eyebrows suggestively and saw a flame ignite in his dark eyes. He grinned.

'Oh *yes!*'

His smile broadened and settled into the lines and creases of his lovely face.

'*There* you are,' she said.

She took him by the hand and led him up the stairs.

Afterwards, they slept and Rosie knew peace. Tom's slumber was not so restful and he found himself back on the battlefield. He was awoken by an explosion, which flung him out of the bed and onto the floor. His cries roused Rosie and she rushed to his side.

'Get back in the tank!' he screamed at her.

She cradled his head and stroked his damp hair.

'Hush my darling, it's not real.'

'The enemy,' he panted, 'the enemy's approaching. RUN!'

'Look at me, Tom. It's Rosie.'

He looked at her.

'Rosie?'

She nodded.

'You're at home with me.'

He sat up and looked around the bedroom.

'I am?'

'Yes.'

'Is the war over then?' he asked.

'Yes darling, it's over.'

He let out a loud whoop.

'Shush!' she laughed, 'you'll wake the neighbours.'

The last thing she wanted was one of those busybodies knocking on the door. She got up.

'Shall we have breakfast?'

Tom got up too but then flopped down onto the bed.

'I'm still tired,' he said, 'how about you?'

He patted the empty space beside him on the mattress and she giggled.

'I could do with forty winks myself,' she said and lay down next to him.

They cuddled, oblivious to all else but the muted delight of their whispered intimacy. Oblivious to the bedroom door slowly opening and a shadowy figure entering the room.

Chapter Two

Rosie didn't notice the intruder until it was too late. She screamed at Tom to get out of the way, but he was already being dragged from the room.

'Get off him!' she shrieked. 'Leave him alone!'

Rosie ran out onto the landing, just in time to see Tom being frog-marched into another bedroom. She chased after them.

'What are you doing with my husband?' she demanded as she burst into the room.

Tom was on the bed, hot tears streaming down his face.

'My *wife,*' he cried and held out his arms to her.

'Tom… Tom,' sobbed Rosie.

The bastard who'd separated them turned to look at her. His ape-like face was contorted in a terrifying grimace. He took a step towards her.

'*Please* Rosie, don't go upsetting him again!' he said.

She felt a hand on her shoulder.

'Now come on, Rosie, don't be so silly.'

It was the *chief* busybody.

'It's OK, Boris,' Busybody told the gorilla, 'I'll take her back to her own room.'

'No,' said Rosie sullenly. 'I want to be with Tom'.

'You know you're not allowed in each other's bedrooms before breakfast,' said Busybody. 'Wait until later and you can make the beds together. You both enjoy that, don't you?'

Rosie didn't like the way Busy spoke to her, all syrupy-sweet, as if she were a child, or an idiot. Or both.

'I want to be with my husband,' insisted Rosie.

'Please don't start all that again,' said Busy as she led Rosie back across the landing. 'Tom's not your husband. He's a resident, like you.'

What was the silly cow saying? Not her husband? Of course he was! She could remember the day they'd married, as clearly as if it were yesterday. Then he'd gone off to fight the Jerries and she'd waited for him to come home. Well, now she'd got him back, *no-one* was going to keep them apart! She sat down in her armchair and regarded Busy coldly.

'Are you saying I don't know my own husband?'

Busy looked her up and down and shook her head.

'Have you been out in the garden in your night clothes again? For goodness sake, Rosie, the bottom of your nightdress is sopping wet!'

Rosie shrugged.

'A bit of rainwater never hurt anyone.'

'Try telling me that when you've got pneumonia!'

'Don't change the subject,' said Rosie huffily.

Busy hunkered down before her and looked her in the eye.

'And what *subject* is that, Rosie?'

'Well, obviously it's... I...'

Rosie paused mid retort. She knew she had something important to say, but couldn't quite put her finger on what it was. Busy smiled maddeningly. What was the stupid woman grinning at? Rosie got up and began to walk back and forth across the bedroom floor. She was upset, she was *very* upset. She wanted... she wanted... what in blazes *did* she want? There was a soft knock on the door and another busybody came in.

'Morning Rosie,' she said.

Rosie stopped pacing and squinted at her. It was the pretty one. Slim, young, with blonde hair like rope, hanging down her back in great bulky coils.

'You OK?' asked Blondie.

'Course she is,' sniffed Busy.

'I was asking Rosie,' said Blondie evenly.

'Fine,' said Busy, '*you* deal with her.'

And with that she flounced out the room. Blondie guided Rosie back into her chair.

'Shall I do your hair?' she asked.

Rosie nodded, but found that she could not speak.

'Let's get you dressed first. You're shivering.'

Rosie noticed with surprise that she was indeed trembling from head to toe. It was that stupid woman's fault, she thought, the one that had just left. She couldn't remember her name, or even her face. Just that she always put her in a bad mood. Blondie picked out an outfit and helped her into the skirt. Rosie accepted her assistance with the fiddly zip, but insisted on doing up the buttons of her blouse herself.

'You have such pretty hair,' said Blondie when they were done, 'like a shiny silver halo.'

Rosie put her hand to her head. She had always loved her hair. Blondie hummed while she brushed it, a happy, upbeat tune that Rosie had never heard before.

Down in the dining room, Tom was helping one of the other busybodies set the tables for breakfast. He was humming too when Rosie walked in and she was pleased to see him so cheerful. She chose a table by the window and waited for him to join her.

'Morning,' he said shyly, as he slipped into the chair opposite.

She smiled at his bashful expression. He hadn't changed a bit since the day they'd met.

'How do I look?' she asked. She was wearing her favourite skirt and blouse and Blondie had done a good job on her hair.

'Lovely,' said Tom. 'You always look lovely,' he added.

Rosie was pleased.

'Do you want to help me make the beds after?'

'That sounds nice.'

They ate their toast in silence, but she noticed Tom casting curious furtive glances in all directions.

'Are you alright, darling?' she asked.

He wiped his mouth on a napkin and folded it neatly before placing it next to his plate.

'Yes, yes. It's just…'

'Yes?'

She smiled at him encouragingly.

'Can I ask you a question?' asked Tom.

'Anything, my love.'

He looked about the dining room again and she followed his gaze, taking in the pub-style bar and the numerous formally decorated dining tables.

'Is this our house?'

'Yes. This is where we live.'

'Well then.' He paused and lowered his voice. 'Who are all these people?'

She looked at the elderly ladies entering the dining room, arm-in-arm and at the old gent sitting on his own with his head in his hands. To be honest, she wasn't sure who they were either. She knew that they lived here too, but was confused as to why. And why were they all so old? Surely a young married couple such as themselves should be living alone in a nice terrace somewhere.

'I, I don't know,' she faltered. 'I'm sorry.'

'Why are you sorry, sweetheart?' he asked, his voice tinged with loving concern.

'Because I don't know.'

He seemed puzzled.

'What don't you know?'

She thought about it for a moment, took his hand across the table and giggled.

'I don't know.'

Chapter Three

That afternoon, Rosie decided to spend time with her "smell collection", an assortment of vials, tubs and canisters which she kept for their evocative properties. She went to her closet and, taking down the shoe box which housed her collection, laid everything out in a neat line on the bedroom floor. Her favourite item, an old can of shaving foam with a distinctive odour, she usually used only sparingly. However, today she felt an intense need to bring to mind her father and so squirted a large creamy mound onto her hand and breathed in its soapy perfume. Next she picked up a little tub of beeswax, which she held under her nose and which transported her back to her childhood bedroom. Her lavender water, she saved until last. She owned several bottles of the fragrance, which she liberally daubed herself with every morning, but there was one special bottle which *exactly* recreated the smell of her own body the day she first kissed Tom. She pulled out the stopper now and, inhaling deeply, was rewarded with an intoxicating plethora of giddy feelings and memories. She remembered *everything* about that day and, as she sniffed her precious fragrance, she allowed her mind to travel back there now.

Rosie examines herself in her mother's gilt-edged mirror. She looks beautiful, even by her own high standards. The crimson in her cheeks makes a pleasing addition to her usually creamy-white palette and her blue eyes twinkle with the excitement of being desired by a handsome man. She sighs dreamily as she thinks of Tom; his strong body, his baby blond curls, his hazel-coloured eyes and shy smile. A rustle of a skirt in the doorway warns her that her mother has entered the room.

'Rosalind, are you wearing rouge?'

Rosie's eyes flick up to find her mother staring at her in the mirror.

'No Mother,' she replies, casting her eyes downwards in a manner more becoming of the daughter of a senior government official. Her mother often reminds her that her father's "higher occupational position" means her behaviour must be, at all times, unimpeachable. Although she tries hard to please her parents, Rosie finds this expectation almost impossible to live up to. Now that she has fallen in love, she is going to have to break a few house rules and the prospect of this both thrills and terrifies her in equal measure.

'Then are you ill?' her mother enquires as Rosie turns to face her.

'No... why do you think—?'

Her mother grabs her roughly by the chin and scrutinises her face.

'You're very flushed. Do you have a temperature?'

'I'm fine Mother, really!'

'Go to bed.'

She nods for emphasis, certain that this is the correct course of action.

'Wh-at?!'

'Go to your bed and lie down. I'll call the doctor.'

Rosie's heart begins to race. No, no, no! If she goes to bed now, she will never be able to get a message to Tom in time and their rendezvous is in half an hour!

'But I was on my way to Lillian's,' she begins, 'she has a knitting pattern for me. You said I could.'

Rosie tries hard not to sound petulant. Nothing angers her mother more than a show of defiance.

'When I said you could go, I was not in full possession of the facts. Now that you are ill, I have changed my mind.'

'But, I'm not ill,' cries Rosie, knowing the battle is already lost. Even if her mother accepts she is well, she will send her to her room for answering back. On cue, her mother pales and begins to tremble, a sure sign that an eruption is soon to follow.

'Rosalind,' she begins.

Rosie saves her the trouble of frogmarching her up the stairs. She flees from the room and up to her bedroom, locks herself in and flings herself face down on the mattress. Moments later her mother tries the door, rattling it furiously when she realises it is bolted.

'Open the door this second, Rosalind!'

Rosie sits up, surprised by the ferocity of her mother's rage. She had only meant to lock herself in, not to lock her mother out. But as she rises to open the door, the realisation hits her so hard, that it almost knocks the breath out of her. She is out of her mother's reach.

'I told your father to remove the lock!' her mother shrieks. 'He's far too soft on you!'

The shocking daringness of Rosie's plan is utterly immobilising and so she decides not to think about it. Instead, she pushes open the sash window and scrambles down the oak tree outside her bedroom, colliding with her childhood swing which hangs from its branches. The swing continues to sway back and forth long after she has disappeared into the balmy afternoon haze.

'Rosie?'

Busy stood in the doorway, her hands on her hips.

'Don't you ever knock?' asked Rosie crossly. She hadn't even got to the part where she kissed Tom.

'I'm a busy lady,' said Busy.

'Don't I know it,' grumbled Rosie.

'What's that?'

'I said… good manners cost nothing,' said Rosie, putting down the bottle of scent.

'Get up off the floor!' snapped Busy.

She took Rosie by the arm and hauled her to her feet, letting go before she had fully gained her balance. Rosie pitched forward and caught the top of her leg on the bedpost, thinking it strange that getting up off the floor seemed so difficult nowadays.

'You shouldn't be sitting on the bloody floor at your age,' barked Busy, as if reading her mind.

Rosie shrugged.

'I *always* sit on the floor,' she muttered, rubbing her bruised leg.

'Yeah. Just like you *always* go out in the garden without your shoes on.'

'I like the feel of the wet grass.'

'Are you hurt?' asked Busy. 'Let me see your leg.'

'Certainly not,' sniffed Rosie.

Busy rolled her eyes.

'Come on then, you've got a visitor.'

Rosie was immediately apprehensive.

'What visitor?'

'Your granddaughter. Now, don't be difficult and come with me.'

Granddaughter? *Granddaughter*? Was Busy trying to be funny?

'I don't have a granddaughter,' Rosie told her.

Busy laughed humourlessly, took her firmly by the arm and led her downstairs.

The lady was in the living room, sitting in one of the comfy chairs in the big bay window. She gave Rosie a huge smile as if they were long-lost sisters, but Rosie knew she had never met her before in her life.

'Hi Nan,' she said.

'Is this some kind of joke?' asked Rosie.

'No Nan,' replied the lady. 'I'm Meg, your granddaughter.'

Rosie drew closer and looked her up and down through narrowed, suspicious eyes.

'Can I ask you a question?'

'Of course.'

'Who are you *really*?'

'I'm your granddaughter,' repeated the stranger.

'Right, right. So how old are you?'

'Forty-one.'

Rosie laughed out loud at this. Now she *knew* it was some sort of prank.

'I don't think so, dear.'

'I *am*, Nan,' insisted the lady.

'Well can you please tell me how it's possible that I have a forty-one-year-old granddaughter, when I myself am only forty-five?'

'Mum says she'll pop over on Wednesday,' said the lady, ignoring the question.

'Do I know her?' asked Rosie.

'Sometimes,' said the lady mysteriously.

Rosie shrugged. She had no time for playing silly games.

'It was nice meeting you, dear, but my husband's waiting for me, so if you don't mind – '

The lady's jaw dropped open.

'Your *who*?'

There was something about her which seemed familiar, but Rosie was too distracted to work out what it was.

'Nan, what *are* you –?'

Rosie held up her hand.

'Good-bye, dear.'

The lady opened and closed her mouth in a fishy, indignant sort of way. Like a sturgeon in high dudgeon, thought Rosie and she smiled at her most gratifying play on words.

'A sturgeon in high dudgeon, a sturgeon in high dudgeon, a sturgeon in high dudgeon,' she repeated gleefully to herself as she wandered off to find Tom.

Chapter Four

Tom was confused. The woman sitting next to him said she knew him, but he wasn't so sure. She looked at him as if she wanted him to speak, but he didn't know what to say.

'Right, right. Very nice,' he eventually settled upon.

She seemed like a nice lady and he didn't want to disappoint her. She dabbed at her eyes with a handkerchief, but he could see no tears. An old man sitting opposite them got up and hobbled over. He offered the lady a toffee from a crumpled paper bag and she thanked him, but didn't take one. The old man left the room and Tom felt panicky because now he was on his own with her. She turned back to him.

'*Try* to think, Tommy,' she said, 'for *me*!'

He nodded and smiled, hoping this would be enough to pacify her. He hated to see a woman in distress.

'You remember me?' she exclaimed.

Oh dear, thought Tom, is this some sort of guessing game? He'd never been any good at guessing games, especially charades, which had always been the scourge of Christmas for him.

'Are you… my sister?' he tried tentatively.

The woman let out a loud groan and took out her handkerchief again. Then suddenly she got up and headed for the door.

'Stay here,' she commanded as she left the room.

She seemed pleasant enough, but rather bossy in Tom's opinion. While he waited for her to return, his wife walked in. His lovely, lovely wife.

'Hello, my darling!' he greeted her.

He blew her a kiss and she blew him one back.

'I'll get a book and join you, sweetheart,' she said going over to the bookshelf.

Tom felt better now that she was in the room and he began to relax a little. The bossy lady came back with a woman in a nurse's uniform. He hoped he wasn't sick. They sat either side of him on the sofa.

'Everything OK, Tom?' asked the nurse.

'I think so,' he replied.

'Jayne says you're a bit out of sorts?'

'Yes. Yes I think I rather am,' he replied absently.

'He's been having a few nightmares recently,' the nurse told the bossy lady.

'He dreams about the war,' added his wife from across the room, 'cries in his sleep sometimes, poor lamb.'

The lady turned white and got slowly to her feet. His wife put her chosen book under one arm and headed towards the sofa.

'And how, may I ask, do *you* know?' asked the pale, trembling woman, barring her passage.

His wife laughed.

'Because I sleep next to him, of course.'

The woman began to splutter and then emitted a high-pitched screech. Tom jumped up in terror. He clutched his wife's outstretched hand and pulled her to him, putting his other arm protectively around her shoulder. Together they stared at the crazy woman's ashen face and horrible gaping mouth and she stared back, her eyes locked on their tightly linked hands.

Rosie was hugely offended by the stranger's outburst. What was *wrong* with the woman? And why was she so outraged? What did she *expect*? Separate bedrooms? She knew they were getting on a bit, but there was nothing wrong with a man and his wife sharing a bed, no matter how old they were. What was the

old biddy up to *now* and what was she shouting about?
Busybodies began running towards them from all directions.

'Will somebody *please* get rid of her!' the woman screamed.

Rosie looked around the room. Who was she talking about?

'Come on Rosie, let's see what's on TV,' said one of the busybodies. It was Blondie. Rosie liked Blondie.

'OK'.

Was it time for *Corrie*? *Corrie* was her favourite soap. She turned to Tom.

'Coming, sweetheart?'

Blondie took Rosie to one side and smiled at her kindly.

'Tom needs to stay here, Rosie,' she said, 'with his wife.'

Rosie shook her head. Had she heard correctly? His *wife*? She pulled away from Blondie.

'*I'm* Tom's wife, you daft cow!'

'*Just get her out of here!*' bawled the mad woman.

Tom began to cry.

In the TV room, Blondie sat Rosie down and tried to talk to her.

'Look Rosie, Tom's new here and he's still very confused. His wife loves him and seeing you two together is making her sad. I know it's hard for you to understand, but you *must* try.'

Blondie was a nice young lady; the only busybody who ever really bothered to explain things to her. So Rosie tried to focus on what she was saying, but honestly, she couldn't make head or tail of it.

'Tom's my husband,' explained Rosie slowly. 'I love him and he loves me. We belong together.'

Blondie sighed.

'I know *you* think that,' she said.

'I know it,' said Rosie simply, 'Tom too.'

'And Tom too,' conceded Blondie.

Rosie looked her squarely in the eyes.

'So if I say he's my husband and *he* says he's my husband…'

She left her unfinished sentence hanging in the air between them. So simple, so *obvious* that it needed no further clarification.

Blondie held up her hands in surrender.

'OK, OK. I get it.'

Chapter Five

Gemma had feared that Jayne Hancock's rage would culminate in a spectacular display of hysteria, but the elderly lady's abrupt switch to seething restraint was somehow much worse.

'So, she thinks my Tom is *her* Tom?' repeated Jayne quietly.

Gemma shifted uncomfortably in her seat.

'That's about the long and short of it, I'm afraid.'

Why had she agreed to cover Mel's shift? Mel was a terrible manager and she was a skiving cow to boot, but at least when she was here it was up to her to deal with any crises. Unfortunately today, that responsibility lay with Gemma as, with Mel off sick, *she* was the most senior member of staff on site. Accustomed as she was to the residents' meltdowns, relatives required more careful handling.

'And Tom… who does he think she is?' asked Jayne.

'His wife… I think.'

'But *I'm* his wife.'

Oh God, thought Gemma, any second now she's going to lose it.

'I know. This must be very upsetting for you.'

Jayne's lips began to move soundlessly and Gemma looked away discreetly while she recomposed herself.

'He recognised me last week,' whispered Jayne.

Gemma nodded and volunteered her most sympathetic smile.

'He… he remembered my name, where we lived. We talked about the geraniums he'd planted in the garden.'

Gemma searched her mental stockpile of soothing platitudes.

'With dementia, there are often moments of lucidity.'

She'd heard that one on *Casualty* and liked the air of wisdom and professionalism it gave her. Disappointingly, Tom's wife remained stubbornly indifferent to her best line.

'Why? *Why*? Why me?' she was now muttering, her eyes fixed on a point above Gemma's head.

Gemma sighed and ran her fingers through her hair. She liked working here, *loved* the plush surroundings and the unlimited tea and coffee, but there were far too many competing egos to negotiate. The residents and their families were all so damned demanding and self-absorbed. With relief, she saw the office door open and Chrissie's unmistakable blond dreadlocks swing into view.

'Sorry to interrupt, thought you could use—'

Gemma motioned her in and pointed to a chair in the corner. Mrs Hancock blanked Chrissie and began to stare intently at Gemma, through cold, red-rimmed eyes.

'You're going to have to keep them apart!' she barked.

Startled, Gemma jumped up and turned to her colleague.

'Fine. No problem,' she agreed, 'we can do that, can't we Chrissie?'

'We can?'

Chrissie didn't look too convinced. Gemma scowled at her and then smiled at Jayne.

'Well obviously, not all the time,' she said, 'but we can make sure they're never left alone together.'

Chrissie cleared her throat and Gemma shot her another warning glance.

'I was thinking,' began Chrissie, 'that, with Mrs Hancock's support, we could work something out to avoid any further distress to Tom and Rosie.'

Gemma felt like throttling the stupid little tart. Jayne looked at Gemma in horror.

'What *is* she suggesting? That they be allowed to play husband and *wife*?'

She spat out the word "wife" with furious rancour.

'No, of course not!' assured Gemma. She turned to glare at the young care worker. '*Are* you, Chrissie?'

Chrissie sighed. It was at times like this that she wished she didn't have one of those annoying pricking-type consciences. Without it, she could choose to either lie effortlessly to Mrs Hancock, or to cheerfully agree a course of action which would cause pain and suffering to a sweet elderly couple. Either option would resolve the current dilemma quickly and easily, but neither was acceptable to her infuriating sense of justice.

'The thing is,' she tried again, 'they have a genuine fondness for each other, so I was thinking that – '

'I've heard quite enough, *thank you*!' said Jayne. She stood and turned to Gemma. 'I'm going home now and I'm taking my husband with me.'

'For a visit?' asked Gemma.

'Permanently.'

She picked up her bag and turned smartly on her heel.

Chrissie looked at Gemma, who gave a "who-are-we-to-stop-her?" shrug. Chrissie shook her head and, pushing back her chair with a loud scrape, got to her feet.

'I'm afraid we can't let you do that, Mrs Hancock.'

Jayne froze, her hand on the door handle.

'What are you saying?' she said slowly.

Chrissie took a deep breath.

'I'm saying that we would be unable to release Mr Hancock back into your care at this present time.'

Jayne whirled around to face Chrissie.

'*How dare you!*' she hissed.

Chrissie held up her hands.

'Both social services and your GP were involved in the decision-making process— '

Jayne took several rapid steps towards her and banged her fist on the desk.

'Who in *God's* name do you— ? '

'And as Mr Hancock doesn't have the mental capacity to make the decision,' continued Chrissie, raising her voice above that of the enraged relative before her, 'it was decided that a nursing home was in his best interest.'

'You jumped-up *little*— '

'You stated at the time,' persisted Chrissie firmly, 'that you were no longer able to cope with his day-to-day care needs.'

'He *soiled* his bed, for crying out loud,' roared Jayne, 'who in their right mind would be able to cope with *that*?'

Jayne's face was so close to Chrissie's that Chrissie could see the tiny thread-veins on her nose and could detect the faintest whiff of wine on her breath. The monstrous Mrs Hancock, a woman with the meticulously well-groomed facade of a death-mask, became suddenly vulnerable and human. Chrissie saw tears amassing in her eyes and felt a sudden rush of compassion towards her.

Grudgingly, Gemma gave Chrissie an admiring sidelong glance. Where had she learnt all that stuff? She sounded like a proper legal eagle. Maybe she should start watching less *Casualty* and more *Judge Judy*, so that she too could swot up on the lingo. To Gemma's intense relief, Mrs Hancock was now blubbing. Tears she could cope with! She would now be able to intervene in a manner befitting her professional position. She placed herself in between the two other women.

'Please sit down, Mrs Hancock,' she said grandly.

Jayne collapsed back into the chair she had recently vacated. Gemma turned to Chrissie and waved her away, indicating that, as senior carer, she was now taking charge. Chrissie smiled, but infuriatingly refused to shift. Instead she walked around Gemma and crouched down in front of Jayne. She put her hand gently on her shoulder.

'I'm so sorry, Mrs Hancock but Gemma and I… well, we can't make those sorts of decisions. Under the circumstances, we'd need to seek expert advice.'

Jayne sighed; an involuntary, shuddering sob of a sigh.

'At the end of the day,' continued Chrissie, 'we all just want what's best for Tom, don't we?'

Jayne turned to look at her and gave an almost imperceptible nod.

'I'm tired,' she said, eventually. 'We'll talk about this… this *other woman* next time.'

'Of course,' agreed Chrissie.

'Goodbye,' said Jayne, extending her hand.

After Jayne had gone, Gemma considered giving Chrissie a ticking-off for her insubordination, but thought better of it. After what she'd just witnessed, she didn't fancy her chances in an argument against the verbally nimble young upstart. Anyway, there was a slim chance that she actually did have some sort of legal training, although, with her weird tribal tattoos and that ridiculous matted hair, she didn't look the type.

'How do you know that stuff?' asked Gemma, her curiosity getting the better of her.

'What stuff?' asked Chrissie. 'About Tom, you mean?'

Gemma nodded.

'It's quite simple, really.'

Chrissie crossed the room to a large cabinet, took out a bulging folder and threw it on the desk.

'I bothered to read his file.'

Chapter Six

Rosie couldn't find Tom anywhere. He wasn't in his bedroom, or hers. He wasn't sitting under the oak tree or reading his paper in the lounge. She ambled into the kitchen and watched two of the busybodies as they busied themselves with dinner. Busy, always busy, thought Rosie, glumly. One of them looked up, his hand shoved half-way up a chicken.

'Alright Rosie?'

'Where's Tom?' she asked.

The busybody shrugged and returned his attention to the hapless fowl.

'He was helping me peel the veggies,' offered the other, 'but then he wandered off.'

'Anyway,' resumed the chicken-stuffer, 'you're not supposed to be hanging out with him anymore, are you?'

Much to Rosie's annoyance, he waggled the index finger of his free hand at her, as one would a naughty schoolgirl.

'Not supposed to be *hanging* out with him,' repeated Rosie incredulously, but she decided not to push it. She had better things to do with her time than to argue with Peel and Stuffer.

Back in her bedroom she sat down on the bed and looked out across the garden. She placed her hands on the windowsill and laid her chin upon them. Her tired eyes rested on the daffodils, which waved in greeting, their pretty heads dipping and stretching on the breeze. She felt a sudden need to feel that same wind on her face and pulled the window handle upwards, pushing the button to release the catch. It didn't budge.

'That's strange,' mumbled Rosie.

She was *sure* the window had opened easily that very morning and so she tried again, this time with an added shoulder barge, which she threw her full weight behind. She slipped down onto the bed, clutching her damaged arm and catching a glimpse of the oak tree at the bottom of the garden, its drowsy limbs lurching listlessly back and forth. How weary it looks, she thought. When she was a girl, she had often drawn strength from its sturdy branches, which had stretched proudly past her bedroom window.

'When did we get so old and tired, my friend?' she murmured tearfully into her pillow.

Rosie's oak tree soon becomes an unwitting collaborator in her first tender clandestine relations with Tom. As well as being a handy nocturnal escape route for Rosie, it also provides Tom with the means to reach his sweetheart's bedroom. The first time she sees his leg emerging from the shadowy branches and appearing through the open window, she fears she will faint with nervous excitement, delight and the delicious anticipation of illicit pleasures to come. He stands before her in all his masterful, masculine glory and she fights the urge to push him back out into the inky blackness beyond her girlhood sanctuary. She regards him through downcast lashes.

'H... hello,' she stammers.

His smile droops and his overall demeanour becomes a little less cocksure.

'You're not having second thoughts are you?' he asks.

'Maybe. A bit,' she confesses.

'Why?' he asks, sounding genuinely perplexed.

'Well, firstly my parents would disown me if they ever found
— *'*

'They won't,' he cuts in, 'they're happily dancing the night away at the Lord Mayor's Ball, so we've got at least three hours to—'

'Then there's my... my—'

He takes her hand and gives her a look so intense that it commands full eye-contact.

'Rosalind May Dewitt, I am hopelessly in love with you. I want us to be together forever and I will do my best to make you happy, if you'll let me.'

She'd fantasised, visualised, hoped, prayed and dreamed for this moment, but now that it is happening, she is suddenly beset by doubt. She shakes her head.

'I, I don't know—'

'You don't feel the same?'

'Of course I do! You know I do.'

'Then give me one good reason why we shouldn't be together.'

'I can think of millions!'

He seems amused. 'I'm listening.'

'Well, number one, the obvious one, there's my reputation.'

'We're going to get married, so that settles that one.'

He moves closer to her.

'Then, you said it yourself, I could fall pregnant!'

He laughs.

'I'll be careful.' He takes another step towards her. 'And I'd marry you anyway,' he adds with a devilish grin.

'I know this must sound awfully childish,' she gushes, 'especially when I've been so very keen until now, but I can't help but be nervous. I'm sorry if I'm being ridiculous, but there it is and, really, I'm—'

He takes her in his arms and silences her with a kiss.

The sound of persistent knocking seeped into Rosie's dream and she reluctantly opened her eyes. She'd been entangled in the sheets of her girlhood bed, tingling under the touch of Tom's

wandering fingers and gasping for more of his salty kisses. He'd
been on the point of removing her underwear and she yearned to
return to this, their first intimate encounter, but now that she was
awake, she couldn't ignore the knocking, or the throbbing pain
in her shoulder. She racked her brain, but couldn't recall what
she'd done to it. She thought she remembered it was something
to do with the old oak. Maybe she'd fallen out of it? Her mother
was always telling her off for climbing trees.

'Rosie?'

She raised her head sleepily from her pillow.

'Mother?' she called.

The door opened and her mother padded across the room to
her bedside. Rosie sat up.

'What have you done to your hair?' she asked.

'Nothing. It's the same as it's always been.'

Rosie stared at her mother's hair in confusion. It was blond,
tangled and strange, not at all the sort of style she usually
sported.

'You're not my mother,' concluded Rosie.

The young woman smiled.

'No, I'm Chrissie,' she said. 'Been having a nap?'

Rosie sat up and winced in pain. Chrissie sat on the end of
the bed, a look of concern in her eyes.

'What's wrong?'

'I've hurt my shoulder,' she said.

'Maybe you've slept on it funny?' suggested the young
blond.

'Maybe.'

'Do you want me to take a look?'

Rosie shrank away from her. The last thing she wanted was a
complete stranger poking and prodding her. Blondie pulled
back.

'It's dinner time,' she said gently, 'do you want to come
down?'

'What is it?' asked Rosie.

'Roast chicken. Hungry?'

Rosie was hungry. But not for roast chicken.

'Just leave me alone,' she said and slumped back down onto the bed.

Blondie opened her mouth to say something but thankfully thought better of it. Instead she got up and headed for the door.

'I'll bring you up a chicken sandwich later,' she said.

Rosie ignored her. Maybe if she closed her eyes, she'd go back into the lovely dream. Tom had been there and… she sat bolt upright in bed.

'Where's Tom?' she called.

Blondie turned in the doorway and looked at her sadly.

'He's having dinner in his room tonight.'

'I want to see him,' said Rosie.

'Tomorrow,' said Blondie, 'I promise.'

Tomorrow, thought Rosie forlornly. *Tomorrow*. Didn't Blondie know that tomorrow never comes?

Chapter Seven

Before she left for the evening, Chrissie checked on Tom one last time. He'd spent most of the evening crying in his bedroom, refusing food or drink and asking for his wife. Chrissie was relieved to see that he was now snoring softly, the emotional trauma of the day clearly etched on his lined features. She closed the door quietly behind her, glad at least that he'd found temporary respite from his pain and confusion. On her way out, she let herself into the office and checked the rota. Gemma was on nights for the rest of the week, thank goodness. Chrissie was on days, so it meant she could sneak into Rosie's bedroom first thing and usher Tom out if necessary. If she was caught, she'd be in seriously hot water, but at least with Gemma out the way, she had a week's grace to come up with a more long-term plan. She was glad she didn't have to see Gemma for selfish reasons too. Until today, they'd disliked, yet tolerated each other, but she knew she'd made an open enemy of her now. Not that she cared what bigoted hypocrites like Gemma thought of her. Christina Barclay-Holmes had never sought or courted the approval of her peers. She paid no heed to public opinion and enjoyed her carefully cultivated reputation as a misfit because it allowed her a certain anonymity. She liked the fact that people like Gemma Noakes didn't know what to make of her; that they were baffled by the incongruity of her dreadlocks and posh accent. The *real* people, the people that needed her, those that actually mattered, they saw past her disguise and into her heart. They understood the simple truth of her caring nature and allowed her the freedom to be herself. Her thoughts turned to Rosie, the most complicated and fascinating of all the home's residents. They'd formed such a close bond in the six months that Chrissie had been here, but in the weeks since Tom's arrival, she'd felt her slipping away out of her reach. She hadn't yet made up her mind if Tom's resemblance to Rosie's dead husband and the subsequent profound effect this had had on the elderly lady was a good or a bad thing. Rosie had been perfectly content before Tom moved in; surrounded by her treasured "smell collection" and knick-knacks, taking early morning constitutionals in the garden, talking to the trees and flowers and enjoying regular visits from her daughter and grandchildren. Of course, there had been times when she'd been confused and frustrated, days when she hadn't known her daughter or even been able to remember her own name; that was just part and parcel of dementia. At least she hadn't been suffering the way she was now. But then, thought Chrissie, was suffering really such a bad thing? To suffer was to feel, to love, to *be*. Was it really preferable to spend one's twilight days in the comfortable numbness of a half-remembered life? She supposed it all came down to The Bard's immortal question: "To be or not to be?" She knew which one she'd choose.

Chrissie sat down on the swivel chair behind the desk and sighed. She had to admit that for all the anguish Rosie and Tom's relationship was causing, no-one could deny that what they felt for each other was something akin to love. Maybe it was even the real thing. Who knew? And who had the right to tell them what they did or didn't feel or what they did or didn't represent to each other? She knew she didn't feel qualified to make that sort of judgement and she was damned if a small-minded idiot like Gemma Noakes was going to make it for them. It suddenly struck Chrissie as unfair that Rosie and Tom couldn't express their feelings for each other without fear of criticism or reprisals. Why should dementia rob them of their civil liberties as well as their mental faculties? Why should they be forced to sneak around like criminals in the dead of night? Of course, she understood Mrs Hancock's outrage and the earlier outburst from Rosie's indignant granddaughter, but if they wanted to be together, then surely that was their basic human right? Chrissie thought of the man *she* loved and the choices they'd made. True, he was now thousands of miles away and it was doubtful that their relationship would survive, but at least she could jump on a plane if she wanted to. There was nothing keeping her and Steve apart, but a hell of a long distance and his sheer pig-headedness.

On impulse, Chrissie decided that she owed it to Rosie and Tom to do a little research on their behalf and so she took off her coat, put down her bag and switched on the computer.

Whilst she waited for the old dinosaur to boot up, she cast a leisurely eye around the office, with its bulky filing cabinets and notice boards full of ancient NHS posters and messages to employees who had long since left. She noticed with disgust that the keyboard had sandwich crumbs wedged in between its dusty keys; hardly the cutting-edge technology one would expect of a luxury nursing home. At least the residents were well cared-for, she thought, although there was still something about the chaos and decay at the company's operational hub that she found vaguely disturbing. Eventually, she was able to open the intranet and find the policies and procedures document. Scrolling down it, she could find nothing which related specifically to sex and intimacy in the home. She pursed her lips. She had known it was a bit of grey area, but to have no reference to it at all was surely wrong. What if a resident's partner wanted to spend the night, for example? Surely there should be a procedure in place for such an eventuality? It hadn't happened yet, but maybe that was because people were too afraid to ask. If it wasn't mentioned in the Residents Information Pack, then they would probably assume it was prohibited, or at the very least discouraged. Chrissie shook her head, beyond disappointed. Her employers were certainly not about to win any awards for modern views and enlightened attitudes. The taboo surrounding sex and the elderly was clearly just too strong.

Rosie's eyes flew open. Someone was in her bedroom. She watched as the spectral figure moved about the room, feeling its way with shadowy hands.

'Who's there?' she whispered.

'It's me. Tom.'

Relief flooded through her and she switched on the bedside lamp. His eyes glowed with passion across the hazy pool of light.

'Hello darling,' he said.

'You nearly gave me a heart attack,' she replied sternly.

He hung back, looking suitably chastened. She softened and pulled aside her bed covers.

'Are you getting in or what?'

It was all the encouragement he needed.

Speech is pointless; their lips having far more pressing matters to attend to, but their bodies speak to each other in a language beyond words. They connect effortlessly, fitting together and within each other with a fluency born of uncontainable fervour. They navigate one another's bodies expertly, with only their mutual empathy and soft moans of ecstasy for guide. And when they stop to rest, clasped together in a tight embrace, the Morse code of their accelerated heartbeats transmits passion and feeling from deep within their unified core.

Afterwards, enfolded in his powerful arms with her head on his muscular chest, she feels tinier than ever, but also, rather wonderfully, more substantial.

'A beautiful paradox,' she murmurs as she kisses his damp skin.

Tom lifts his head from the pillow.

'I'm a what?' he asks.

'A beautiful paradox,' she repeats. 'Well, I am – we are, I mean.'

'Hmmph,' he replies, 'well, whatever I am, I'm tired.' He flops back down, pulling her up the bed so they are facing each other on the pillow. 'So, if it's alright with you, I'm going to

have a quick nap before your parents get home and I have to shinny back down that bloody oak tree.'

She giggles.

'Alright.'

'Good.'

He kisses her tenderly and within minutes is slumbering softly. She watches him for a while, spellbound by his loveliness, and then she too falls into a deep, untroubled sleep.

Chapter Eight

At seven o'clock on the dot, Chrissie tiptoed into Rosie's room. As she'd suspected, Tom had found his way in there during the night and he and Rosie were snuggled up together in her single bed with their arms around each other. To Chrissie, they looked almost angelic; their careworn faces rejuvenated by the healing power of their restful, united sleep. It seemed such a shame to separate them, but it couldn't be helped.

'Tom,' she whispered.

Neither dreamer stirred.

'It's time to get up,' she said more urgently.

Boris would be doing his rounds in fifteen minutes and the last thing her beloved Darby and Joan needed was another rude awakening from that oaf! She shook Tom's arm gently and he opened one eye.

'What is it?' he asked, groggily.

Chrissie's ruse depended heavily on his fondness for the morning paper.

'Your newspaper's just been delivered,' she said as brightly as possible, 'I thought you might like to read it in bed.'

'Oh righto… great.'

He sat up expectantly, nudging Rosie as he did so, but mercifully she didn't open her eyes. Instead she mumbled something incomprehensible under her breath and then turned over with a contented sigh. Chrissie knew she'd have to act fast.

'Oh, err, it's in *your* bedroom,' she faltered, 'I brought it up earlier with a cup of tea.'

'Lovely,' beamed Tom, clambering out of Rosie's bed.

Chrissie felt terrible for manipulating him in this way, but reminded herself that needs must and followed him thankfully across the landing. The moment Tom's door closed behind him, she heard the heavy clump of Boris' feet mounting the stairs. That was a close shave, she thought and vowed to get to work even earlier the following morning.

Rosie stormed into the dining room, eyes ablaze. She collared Chrissie as she was pouring tea for a little old lady with a shaky head and hands.

'Hey you. *Chrissie!*' she spat.

She brought both her fists down on the table with a loud thump, causing the old lady's head to vacillate all the more.

'Where's… my… husband?' growled Rosie slowly and threateningly, her eyes locked on Chrissie's.

The old lady's bottom lip began to wobble. Was *everything* about her wobbly? Rosie gave her a stony glare too for good measure. The young woman edged towards Rosie and placed a hand on her arm.

'Get off me!' roared Rosie, jerking her arm away.

The other busybodies and oldies in the room stared at her, but she didn't care. All she cared about was Tom. Everyone else could go hang!

Chrissie was stunned by Rosie's behaviour and by the fact that she'd actually remembered her name. She usually called her Blondie, or in moments of extreme irritability, Nuisance, but very rarely, if ever, Chrissie. She knew she'd have to tread carefully. Since starting at the nursing home, she'd learned that people with dementia could become very hostile all of a sudden and, much as she liked Rosie, she had no desire to be on the receiving end of aggressive verbal or physical behaviour. She also had Ellen to think about. She was recovering from a stroke and looked terrified, the poor old thing.

'Rosie, I know you're angry,' began Chrissie, as evenly as possible, 'but *believe* me, I'm on your side.'

To her intense relief, she saw the familiar softness return to Rosie's eyes and felt her body slacken beside her.

'I know, I know. I'm sorry.'

Rosie sat down at the breakfast table and smiled sweetly at Ellen.

'Pass the toast, please,' she asked her.

Ellen smiled back but made no attempt to hand over the toast rack.

'The toast please, dear,' repeated Rosie.

Chrissie sat down between them and passed Rosie the toast.

'Ellen can't hear you,' she informed her, 'she's deaf.'

Rosie nodded absently and began to fiddle with the butter knife.

'What am I doing here?' she asked suddenly.

Chrissie was temporarily thrown. It was a question Rosie often asked her, but never with such intensity, as if she *really* wanted an answer this time.

'Well…' began Chrissie.

'Where's Tom?'

Now that one she could answer more easily. Of course, up until three weeks ago, it had been an equally tough subject to navigate. Gone to a better place. Waiting for you in heaven. Watching over you. These had been her stock answers of the past six months. That was definitely an advantage of Tom Hancock's arrival; she could now answer Rosie's eternal question with complete honesty: he's in the garden/kitchen/bedroom etc.

'He's reading his paper in bed,' replied Chrissie.

Rosie jumped up, her toast untouched.

'Rosie, aren't you going to——?'

But she was already gone.

For the rest of the day, Rosie barely left Tom's side. When, after lunch, the chiropodist came to see him, she waited patiently outside his bedroom. Then later, when a meddlesome woman insisted on meeting with her, Rosie was adamant that

Tom should join them too. Blondie introduced the woman as Anne, a nurse.

'So,' began Anne, 'this is the famous Tom you were telling me about last time?'

'Yes, this is my husband,' said Rosie, glowing with possessive pride as she placed a hand on his knee.

Tom leant over and shook the woman's hand.

'Do you want Tom to stay?' she asked.

'Whatever you've got to say to me, you can say in front of Tom,' replied Rosie.

Blondie and the visitor exchanged looks, which immediately got under Rosie's skin.

'My husband and I are quite busy today,' she informed them, 'what is it we can do for you?'

'I've just popped in for a chat,' replied the woman.

'Who are you? Do I know you?' enquired Rosie.

'I'm a nurse. I come to see you every couple of weeks.'

'To take my blood pressure?'

'I'm not that kind of nurse. I help people by talking to them.'

It occurred to Rosie that there was something fishy going on.

'What sort of a nurse is *that*?'

The infuriating woman smiled and Rosie felt the anger rise up inside her again. She turned to Blondie.

'I've got a right to know!'

Tom flinched at the sound of Rosie's raised voice.

'You're not going to take her away from me again are you?' he asked.

'Of course not,' said the stranger. Her voice was low and soothing, like the sound of a rolling wave on a distant beach. 'I've come to see you both today because I want to make sure you're happy, that's all. Are you?'

'Are we what?'

'Happy?'

Rosie couldn't remember ever meeting such a nosey woman in all her life!

'We're perfectly fine,' she sniffed, grabbing Tom's hand.

'Well, that's great!' said Nosey and she looked like she meant it. She picked up a little notebook and wrote something down.

'Well then,' she beamed, settling back in her armchair, 'last time we talked about the daffodils, Rosie, do you remember?'

Rosie squinted her eyes and the conversation came dancing back to her along a beam of light.

'Yes,' she nodded, 'I told you that spring is my favourite season.'

'That's right.'

'Tom left me in winter, but he came back to me in the spring.'

Tom looked up at this.

'I never left you, sweetheart,' he said.

She turned to him.

'Yes you did. You went off to fight Hitler, but you're back now.'

Tom nodded.

'That's right.'

He looked at each of the assembled women in turn.

'I went to war, you know. A long time ago.'

Chrissie smiled and nodded in what she hoped was an appropriate manner. She wasn't sure she liked the turn the conversation had taken, but Anne seemed quite relaxed with it all; she was sitting back with the assured air of a great mediator who had pulled off a diplomatic coup. Chrissie had only met Anne a few times and still didn't know what to make of her. She watched her now as she chatted easily with Rosie and Tom, her keen little eyes gleaming brightly. Are they shining with empathy, thought Chrissie, or is it just the light reflected off her natty designer specs?

'Anyway, you're back now, sweetheart,' Rosie was saying. She patted Tom's hand and turned to Anne. 'It's so nice to have him back.'

'And so everything's going well, then?' asked Anne.

'Of course.' Rosie looked around the room and lowered her voice conspiratorially. 'He's my one-and-only, you know. We're soul mates.'

Anne smiled elusively.

'Can we go now?' asked Rosie.

With Rosie and Tom safely out of earshot, Chrissie made a pot of tea and she and Anne swapped notes.

'So what do you make of it all?' asked Chrissie.

'Well there's a strong bond there, that's for sure,' said Anne, 'but I'm not sure if it's healthy or not.'

'Yes, they've become very dependent on each other,' agreed Chrissie, 'it's difficult to know what to do for the best.'

Anne nodded sympathetically and Chrissie decided to take the plunge.

'You work in quite a few homes, don't you?' she asked.

'Yes.'

'Do any of them have regulations relating to intimacy?'

Anne looked thoughtful.

'Can't say I've ever come across any hard and fast rules, as such, but I'm sure I've read some sort of guide on the subject.'

'Only, I've been doing a bit of research and there's definitely a need for more awareness and training, wouldn't you say?'

'I don't know. I think it's best to use one's common sense in such cases. Above all, we have a duty of care to protect the residents from harm.'

'Of course,' agreed Chrissie and resolved to refrain from further discussion. From her tone of voice, she doubted Anne was the ally she'd hoped for and she'd probably already said too much.

'The thing is,' continued Anne airily, 'most people with dementia aren't really capable of making decisions about sex—'

'Oh, I disagree,' interrupted Chrissie, in spite of herself. 'People with dementia are like any other people. I find that they often understand their own minds as well as anyone else.'

Anne regarded her with interest.

'Are Rosie and Tom in a sexual relationship?'

Chrissie baulked.

'No, no. Of course not, I was talking hypothetically.'

'Good,' said Anne firmly. 'That sort of behaviour should most definitely *not* be encouraged, don't you agree?'

Chrissie smiled and nodded as she cleared away the tea cups, inwardly cursing herself for her indiscretion.

Chapter Nine

Elizabeth approached Greenacres Nursing Home with her habitual feeling of trepidation. As always, she was unsure as to how she would be received, or if she would even be recognised at all. Sometimes her mother knew her and sometimes she didn't; that was just the way it went. It was a tough reality to accept, especially as her mother had always been so quick-witted, even into her eighties. But accept it she must. It was only going to get worse. Today, to add to her general feeling of discomfort, Elizabeth also had Megan's comments on her mind. According to her daughter, her mother had formed a close personal bond with one of the home's male residents. Whether that was true or not remained to be seen, but as Elizabeth entered the grand gabled building, she had a feeling that today's visit was going to be even more testing than usual.

Tom inhaled deeply and held the subtle fragrance within his nasal cavity for as long as possible before exhaling again. He took several more greedy gulps of air before deciding that he would like a more lasting sample of the delightful lavender scent. He sneaked a furtive glance in every direction before wrapping his hand around one of the delicate purple heads and pulling it clean off the stalk. He crushed his illicit prize between his finger and thumb, releasing the imprisoned perfume from the tiny furry grains. He then rubbed his palms together, which had the dual desired effects of dusting the crushed husks from his hands and spreading the scent further and deeper into his skin. Tom's sense of satisfaction far outweighed the guilt he felt at the forbidden act of destroying a flower. He had a sudden sense that he was being watched and looked up towards the house. His wife was on the veranda, observing him with interest. Tom signalled her to join him. She sauntered over with a huge smile on her face.

'Can I have a smell?' she asked.

Before he could answer, she had taken his hand in hers and had begun to nuzzle his palm.

'What are you doing?'

'Having a smell,' she said with a mischievous grin.

'You silly sausage,' he laughed, tickling her cheek tenderly with his lavender infused fingers.

Rosie responded eagerly to Tom's unexpected caress. Grasping his hand, she pressed it to her lips.

'I love you, darling. I do, *I do*,' she breathed.

He traced the shape of her mouth with his index and she felt tiny jolts of electricity go through her. He drew her closer and she looked deep into his eyes. To her surprise, Rosie noticed that they were green; emerald orbs, surrounded by tiny flecks of twinkling silver. Something about his eyes puzzled her and she pulled away from him in confusion.

'Are you alright, sweetheart?' he asked.

Rosie was prevented from answering by the unwelcome appearance of Busy, who came barrelling down the garden path towards them.

'You've got a visitor, Rosie,' she bellowed.

Rosie turned to follow Busy, but something was bothering her. She looked back at Tom, who grinned and gave her a little wave. Rosie was immediately flooded with love for him, but as she trailed Busy back into the house, she couldn't quite shake the feeling that something was amiss.

Chrissie and Jayne were deep in conversation when Gemma swept into the office.

'You can go home now, Chrissie,' she interrupted.

Chrissie looked up and smiled at her sweetly.

'I'll just finish with Mrs Hancock and I'll be off,' she said.

'I can take over,' insisted Gemma.

'No you can't,' said Jayne firmly, 'now if you don't mind, I was having a private word with Miss Barclay Holmes.'

Chrissie felt almost sorry for her red-faced colleague as she shambled back out the room. Almost, but not quite. Gemma slammed the door behind her.

'Awful woman,' muttered Jayne. 'Does she treat them well? Tommy… and the others?'

It was a question Chrissie had often asked herself.

'I think so. I mean, there's no evidence to suggest otherwise,' she answered honestly.

But, she thought to herself, who knows what goes on behind closed doors?

Jayne turned to look out of the window. Chrissie followed her gaze and they were silent for a moment as they watched Tom pottering around the garden in the afternoon sunshine. Chrissie noticed that the light filtering through the trees created a dancing dappled effect on his snowy hair. He looks so much happier than when he first arrived, she mused.

'I chose this place for the garden,' said Jayne. 'Tommy loves trees and flowers, always has.'

Like someone else I know, thought Chrissie.

'I can't say it's an interest we shared,' confessed Jayne. She smiled ruefully. 'I've never been very outdoorsy.'

Looking at her high-heels, pencil skirt and perfect make-up, Chrissie could well believe it. She was the most stylish pensioner she had ever met.

'Neither have I,' confided Chrissie. 'Give me a country club over a country walk any day.'

Their eyes met and Jayne grinned.

'Something tells me you're not really the country club type.'

Chrissie laughed, but gave nothing away.

Jayne felt surprisingly relaxed talking to this unexpected, yet agreeable young confidant. Her general demeanour (notwithstanding the hair of course!) reminded her of her dear sister, one of the few people in her life whose company she had genuinely enjoyed. Since she had now lost both her sister *and* her husband, she had little opportunity for intelligent conversation, or indeed any conversation at all for that matter.

'Poor Tommy,' sighed Jayne, 'I never dreamed it would all end like this.'

'Tom *is* still with us.'

Jayne was stung by the thoughtlessness of Chrissie's comment. She had thought her to be above such insipid clichés.

'*My* Tommy is no longer with us,' she retorted.

Chrissie nodded.

'Of course. I'm sorry.'

Jayne set her mouth in a thin hard line.

'That's what happens when you marry a man fifteen years your senior,' she said with finality, 'he gets old before you do. And dementia is such a debilitating, *humiliating* illness.'

'It can be,' agreed Chrissie.

Jayne leant in towards her.

'Do you know he became obsessed with,' she lowered her voice to a whisper, 'all things to do with his *bowels*.'

Through the hot burn of her shame, Jayne noticed that Chrissie didn't look shocked, or even surprised. It gave her the courage to continue.

'I was preparing breakfast one morning and he came through to ask me what *it* was called. It took me half an hour to work out what he meant. Anyway, that was the beginning of the end.'

She trailed off, beyond mortified, but feeling better for having finally unburdened herself of her heart's most troublesome secret.

Chrissie looked upon Jayne's tortured face. She felt sorry for a woman who could envisage no greater tragedy than her esteemed husband discussing his bowel movements at breakfast. She wondered briefly what Jayne would make of Steve; of his hearty morning farts, his blasé attitude to bodily functions and of his utter lack of regard for either his own, or anyone else's privacy. Despite her best efforts, her thoughts turned to their weekend in a primitive Cambodian beach hut and she was forced to stifle a giggle. She leant over and spontaneously took Jayne's hand.

'Believe me, Tom's in the best place here. We've not seen anything of what you've just described and I was just thinking how much more cheerful he seems recently.'

Jayne sat back in her chair with an irritated "harrumph".

'And I suppose that's all down to this, this *woman*—'

'Rosie,' interjected Chrissie.

'Yes, *Rosie*,' repeated Jayne contemplatively, as if her tongue were trying on the name for size. 'Tommy and Rosie, do they have much in common?'

Chrissie was torn between her desire to answer honestly and her concern for Jayne's feelings.

'Well, they're very similar in age and have a great deal of shared memories about the period before and after the war.'

'I didn't know him then,' said Jayne mournfully.

'No, I suppose you would have been a young girl when the war ended,' agreed Chrissie.

'I must admit, he seemed more alert today,' said Jayne pensively.

Chrissie nodded, hoping that Jayne was slowly coming round to the idea that Tom and Rosie's relationship was mutually beneficial.

'I'm curious,' began Jayne with some difficulty, 'she… *Rosie*… told me that they'd shared a bed. Have they… do they…?'

Chrissie swallowed hard.

'Look. What can I say? I—'

Jayne held up her hand.

'On second thoughts, I don't want to know.'

She got to her feet.

'Well thanks for the tea and chat,' she said briskly, 'I'm going to say goodbye to my husband.'

Chrissie's heart sank. Should she just come right out and ask her? She watched Jayne's retreating frame; proud, erect, exuding moral rigidity. No, she decided, it would be pointless. She had always known it was going to be a long shot, but convincing this stern elderly lady to relinquish her husband into the arms of another woman was turning out to be an impossible task.

Tom's wife had gone back inside with some woman or other. Something to do with a visitor. There were always so many people coming and going; housekeepers, cooks, chauffeurs, cleaners. He wondered how his wife managed to keep on top of it all. Privately, he didn't think they needed quite so much home help, but he wouldn't dream of interfering in her domain.

'I'm off now, Tommy,' said a voice inside his head. Who was Tommy? He thought he recognised the name as his own, but couldn't quite put his finger on the identity of the voice's owner.

'Tommy?'

He whirled around to find an unfamiliar, yet attractive woman standing beside him, smiling at him expectantly.

Jayne studied her husband's handsome face. Chrissie was right; he *did* look much happier.

'See you in two days,' she said.

Tom's eyes widened with a look of sudden recognition, which sent her heart racing with joy and hope.

'Goodbye my dear,' he said, brightly.

She was dizzy with euphoria. Her husband had returned to her! *This* was the man she knew and loved; cheerful, charming, smelling of spring flowers and sunshine. He was nothing like the vacant, disinterested stranger she'd reluctantly grown accustomed to of late. Finally, he'd remembered who she was.

'She's in the house,' said Tom.

'Beg pardon?'

'My wife is in the house,' repeated Tom, 'she'll pay you on your way out.'

'*Pay* me?' echoed Jayne.

Tom's confident smile wavered.

'Aren't you the cleaning lady?'

Jayne opened her mouth to speak, but thought better of it. Instead, she smiled and kissed his cheek.

'Bye Tommy,' she said.

Rosie looked into the pale, tired face of her daughter.

'Hello Elizabeth.'

'I hear you've gone and gotten yourself hitched.'

'Don't talk in riddles please, Elizabeth dear.'

Elizabeth was glad at least that her mother knew her name today and managed to swallow her cutting riposte.

'Who is he?' she enquired.

'Who's who?'

'This new man of yours?'

Her mother shook her head.

'There's no new man. There's only ever been one man for me.'

Elizabeth nodded. She knew that much to be true.

'Meg said you wouldn't see her.'

'Who's Meg?'

'My daughter. Megan. Your granddaughter.'

'You're looking old, Elizabeth.'

'I *am* old, Mum.'

Rosie chuckled.

'You need to take better care of yourself. Use eye cream for those laughter lines.'

Elizabeth pulled at the baggy skin under her eyes. 'There's no moisturiser in the world that's going to get rid of these wrinkles.'

Rosie leant forward and stared intently at her face.

'I'm sorry to hear that, dear. Now whom did you say you were here to see?'

After a dutiful hour of repetitive conversation, Elizabeth was ready to go home. She kissed her mother's paper-thin cheek, which elicited a raised eyebrow and a bewildered shrug, and headed for the exit. On a whim, she stopped a care worker in the doorway and asked her to point out Tom. She was intrigued to know the identity of the man who had stolen her mother's impenetrable heart. The doddery old gent in the slippers was quite a disappointment, but then he was never going to be Clark Gable, she reasoned.

'Apparently he bears more than a passing resemblance to your father,' said the care worker.

'I never knew him,' said Elizabeth. 'He died when I was a baby.'

The care worker nodded sympathetically.

'I'm sorry to sound indelicate,' she began hesitantly, 'but do you mind? About their relationship, I mean?'

Elizabeth had never been very good at "opening up", especially to strangers, but she knew this young hippy woman had some sort of special bond with her mother and she seemed genuine enough.

'No, not really. I mean, if he makes her happy, then who am I to stand in their way?'

The young woman smiled. She seemed unfathomably pleased with this answer. Elizabeth thought this a little odd, but then everything surrounding her mother's unprecedented love affair was odd.

'Odd is becoming the norm, I fear,' she murmured to herself.

She watched her mother cross the room and touch her ancient beau on the cheek. It was a small gesture, which was huge in its significance. Elizabeth had never in all her life seen her mother touch someone with such affection. In fact, for as far back as she could remember, her mother had always done her best to avoid excessive physical contact. Observing her now, holding hands with Tom, she managed to suppress an unanticipated surge of anger, but found that she couldn't quite ignore the child's voice in her head which snivelled petulantly; 'Why him? Why *him*? Why him and not *me*?'

Chapter Ten

Tom awoke with a start. His heart hammered erratically to the sporadic tune of rifle fire in his ears. He tried to speak, but his mouth was full of putrid, blood-soaked mud. With supreme effort, he managed to turn his head to the side and saw the shimmering outline of a woman, smiling beatifically at him. Was he hallucinating? Was this the marvellous invention of a shell-shocked brain as he lay dying?

'Are you back in the land of the living?' asked the apparition beside him.

He stared at her helplessly, not sure how to answer, or even if he was capable of doing so. He pulled at his shirt which was stuck in patches to his damp torso.

'You nodded off for a bit there, love,' she said.

'Nodded off?' he echoed, thickly.

'Yes, during *Emmerdale*. Look, *Corrie*'s on now.'

She nodded towards the TV and he followed her gaze. On the television two people were kissing on the corner of a cobbled street. His wife slipped her hand in his. He squeezed it tightly, holding on for dear life. He was at home, thank God. At home with his wife, watching *Corrie* on TV. Blessed *Corrie*. Blessed, beautiful *Corrie*.

Curled up on the sofa in the staff lounge, Chrissie was surprised that Gemma hadn't hunted her down and shooed her off the premises hours ago. She couldn't face going home just yet. It was bridge night and her mother's awful friends would already be there. She was sick to death of answering questions about her dreads and piercings under the injured gaze of her parents. In fact, since returning home from her gap year, she spent as little time as possible actually *at* home. She took a sip of coffee and logged onto Facebook from her mobile. She needed to see his face again, if only in photos and she longed for news of Cambodia. She clicked on his timeline and read his most recent post:

The children taught me Apsara today (a traditional Khmer dance for women). They thought it was hilarious to see a big burly bloke doing girlie dance moves. Made a right twat of myself but it was worth it to see them all laughing like that. Lol!

Chrissie smiled. How typical of Steve. Making the kids laugh was what he did best; bringing light and humour into the lives of deprived children. She knew just how hard he found life over there, especially since she'd left, and she marvelled at his endless ability to remain upbeat. She sent him a direct message:

Skype tomorrow? Usual time x

She checked her watch. It was three in the morning in Cambodia. She pictured him sleeping soundly in the little staff building in the courtyard and wondered who now occupied the adjoining bedroom. She shook her head, not wanting to dwell too deeply on her replacement at the orphanage. Instead, she turned her attention to his profile picture, which he'd changed yet again. A mock "heroic explorer" pose next to an ancient elephant statue. She immediately recognised it as a photograph she'd taken at the Angkor Wat temple. It had been the perfect day. They'd arrived in Siem Reap the previous afternoon in the back of a pick-up truck and were still riding high on their own intrepidness. She smiled at his silly facial expression; lips pursed, brow knitted, one eyebrow raised in triumph at the "capture" of the huge stone beast. She missed him. She missed his broad Mancunian accent, she missed his overabundance of body hair and, above all, she missed his ridiculous, childlike capacity for joy.

Tom couldn't understand why people felt the need to keep telling him what to do! He was a grown man last time he checked *and* he'd fought for King and country. Surely that gave him the right to make his own decisions about things. The man handed him glass of water.

'Come on, Tom, it's time to take your pills,' he repeated.

'Sorry, but who exactly *are* you?' enquired Tom.

Beside him, his wife giggled. The man turned to her.

'Now look, Rosie, don't you start,' he sighed. 'Gemma'll go mad if she finds you two like this, as it is.'

'What are you talking about?' asked Tom.

'Well, you're all snuggled up together,' began the man, 'and... and you shouldn't really be...' He trailed off. 'Never mind.'

Tom made an irritated, dismissive gesture with his hand.

'Do you mind? I'm trying to watch TV with my wife.'

Rosie lifted her head from his shoulder and gave him an admiring look. The man took a step towards them.

'Take your pills, there's a good man.'

Tom stood and gave back the offending glass of water, spilling some down the front of the man's tabard.

'We're going to bed now,' he informed the exasperated care worker. He held out his hand to Rosie. 'Come on, sweetheart.'

Rosie takes a deep breath, reaches out and grasps his hand. He spins her towards him chuckling, raises his eyebrows suggestively and then twirls her back out again. She throws back her head and whoops with the sheer giddy joy of it, which sends Tom into further fits of laughter. The dance band is wonderful; melodic, lively, life-affirming! The music makes her want to swing her hips and move her feet to the snappy rhythm. So this is a nightclub! She looks around appreciatively. The room is full of young women in pretty georgette dresses and satin shoes, with waves in their hair and trails of young men behind them. She can't believe she's been missing out on such a vital part of her existence for so long. This is where she belongs; with other vivacious, spirited young people.. With music, with laughter. With Tom. As the music comes to a triumphant end,

'I'll never, ever forgive you for as long as I live,' cried Tom.

The cowardly man in the tabard shrugged and the large, pop-eyed woman he'd been to fetch narrowed her eyes.

'I think we can live with that,' she said, taking him by the arm. 'For goodness *sake*, Tom, we can't go through this rigmarole every night.'

He turned to his wife for support, but she was sitting on the sofa, a far-off expression on her face.

'She says I have to go to my own room, sweetheart.'

His wife looked at him with distant, unseeing eyes.

'I, I want to be with you,' he pleaded. 'Sweetheart? Sweetheart?'

The big woman sighed.

'She's having one of her funny turns again.'

'Will she be OK?' asked her colleague.

'Yeah, she'll snap out of it in a bit.'

She turned her attention back to Tom.

'Come on, let's get you upstairs.'

woozy and prays that she won't be sick, not here on the dance floor of the Café de Paris. She cannot make sense of what has just happened. One minute she was dancing in Tom's arms and the next, her father was beside them, prizing them apart with cold, sinewy fingers.

'What is he even doing here?' she mutters to herself.

Has he followed them? She can't imagine that he's here in this popular West End nightspot of his own accord. Not her father! She is bumped from behind by a particularly energetic pair and it propels her into action. Dazedly, she pursues the men across the maple wood dance floor, just as the music comes to an end. On the stage in between the two sweeping staircases, Bert Ambrose and his orchestra make way for an American entertainer. The throngs of dancing couples all move at once, back to their tables on the balcony and at the edge of the dance floor. Rosie is jolted and pushed around the room until she has quite lost her bearings but, by sheer luck, she spots Tom and her father in a shadowy corner behind one of the staircases. As she approaches them, she hears angry words rise above the general buzz and chatter of their convivial surroundings:

'If you've touched a hair on her head, then I'll have you hanging from the gallows before the year's out!'

Rosie reels in shock when she realises the snarling, guttural voice belongs to her father. The violent bully before her bears no resemblance to the gentle, softly-spoken man she knows and loves. She strains to hear Tom's reply, but the American entertainer is singing a silly song and everyone in the room is laughing. She feels sick again. Dizzy and nauseous. Why is she feeling so ill? All she can hear is the ebb and flow of the amplified laughter as it reverberates around her pounding head. The room begins to spin as she takes a wobbly step towards them. She sees Tom sneer and her father's hand fly up to his pale, exposed throat. Again she hears her father's brutish words:

'Look here, you ignorant bastard, what are your intentions towards my daughter?'

'LEAVE HIM ALONE!' roared Rosie.

Tom and Busy turned to stare at her. She grabbed Tom by the hand.

'You're *not* taking him away from me again!'

'Oh, for *fu*... for *crying* out loud, Rosie!'

Busy still had hold of Tom's other arm and gave it an exasperated tug. Tom stumbled towards her, but Rosie pulled him back.

'Well this is great!' yelled Busy. 'This is just *bloody* great!'

Chrissie went to log out of Facebook when Steve's name and photo appeared on the right hand side of the screen.

'What's he doing online at this time?' she mumbled to herself.

She didn't have to wait long to find out as, within seconds, she received a response to her message:

Can't sleep. Come back xxx

She felt tears prick the back of her eyes as she typed her reply:

We've been through all this.

What was the point of prolonging the agony? She loved him, but he'd only ever been after a holiday romance. Or so he said. His reply was instantaneous:

I love you x

The three words she'd so longed to hear now filled the screen of her mobile phone. Bold, black and beautiful. Unanticipated, yet undeniable. Out of the blue, yet out of this world! Through her sobs she heard the ping of another incoming message:

By the way, how're the old codgers?

Chrissie wiped her eyes on the sleeve of her jacket and put away her mobile. She walked out into the hallway, but stopped outside the residents' lounge. Gemma's voice boomed out from behind the closed door.

'For the last time, Rosie, he's *not* your husband!'

Chrissie sighed. She knew she was heading for trouble, but her bothersome conscience was pestering her again. She pushed open the door and saw Tom at the centre of a tug-of-war between Rosie and Gemma. Chrissie quickly assessed the situation: Gemma was holding onto Tom's arm, but Rosie was gripping his hand so tightly that it had gone white. Tom was whimpering in pain and Rosie looked about ready to blow her top. A male carer she barely knew dithered in the doorway, looking helpless and upset.

'Everything OK?' asked Chrissie, as casually as possible.

Gemma let go of Tom's arm and turned on her.

'*You* again!' She took a step towards her, nostrils flaring, eyes flashing dangerously. 'Your shift finished hours ago. Go home!'

Chrissie ignored her and addressed Rosie.

'Let go of Tom,' she said gently, 'you're hurting him.'

Rosie winced and immediately dropped Tom's hand. He massaged it with the other, rubbing life back into the bloodless imprints of Rosie's bony fingers.

'I'm so sorry, sweetheart,' cried Rosie, enfolding him in her arms and kissing his cheek.

'Why don't you go to the kitchen and ask for a cup of cocoa?' suggested Chrissie.

They shuffled out the room, arms interlaced, Rosie murmuring sweet nothings in Tom's ear.

As soon as they were out of earshot, Gemma rounded on Chrissie.

'You think you're so bloody *clever* don't you?' she growled.

Chrissie shrugged.

'Well, it's a good job I was here to diffuse the situation,' she said mildly.

'You sanctimonious little *bitch*!' shrieked Gemma.

Chrissie had had enough. It was time for Gemma to learn a few home truths.

'Do you even *care* about the people you're supposed to be caring for?'

Gemma turned purple.

'What the hell do you know about care work?' she spat. 'I've been doing this job for twenty years!'

Chrissie rolled her eyes. Was she supposed to be impressed?

'For all your clever words and superior, condescending manner, you're nothing but a naive little kid!' Gemma raged.

Chrissie smiled grimly. Gemma's insults would actually be funny, if they didn't sound so pathetically jealous.

'Look, what *is* your problem with Rosie and Tom?' she asked evenly. 'What does it matter that they think they're married? They're not hurting anyone.'

'Apart from his *actual* wife.'

'She'll come round to the idea.'

'Oh I forgot. You and Jayne Hancock are bezzie mates now aren't you!'

Chrissie laughed out loud at this.

'Very mature. Nice.'

'I'll tell you what's not *nice*,' said Gemma slowly, her voice dripping venom, 'encouraging two people with dementia to live in the past. Allowing them to believe in a made-up reality. It's sick!'

Chrissie opened her mouth to reply, but her head began to spin. She sat in an armchair and rubbed her temples, listening to the nagging voice in her head. It was the first time Gemma had ever said anything that made any *sense*.

'I should get going,' she mumbled hoarsely.

Gemma, seeing her mighty adversary floundering, pressed home her advantage.

'I'm sure we'd all be happier living in our own imaginary worlds,' she proclaimed, 'I'd be married to Brad Pitt and chocolate cake would have fewer calories than boiled cabbage!'

She looked down at her young rival and took a moment to appreciate the view from the moral high ground before continuing her sermon. 'But what you'll eventually come to realise is that our residents need to be encouraged to live in the here and now. What you're doing... well, it's just not ethical!'

Gemma got to the end of her edifying discourse and it was all she could do to refrain from punching the air in a triumphant gesture of victory. In terms of language, she'd made *excellent* use of the recent *LA Law* reruns and (the icing on the cake!) she'd managed to emulate the firm but fair manner of her all-time heroine, Jessica Fletcher. The result on Chrissie was quite frankly astounding! She looked at her now; pale, contrite, deferential. *Exactly* as an unqualified carer in her position should be. Gemma sniffed, flicked her hair and made to leave, but couldn't resist a parting shot:

'Just leave the psychology to the experienced care professionals. OK?'

Chrissie flinched at the slamming of the door, but kept staring at the clock on the beige and cream wall in front of her. Beige and cream… calming, pacifying, *numbing*. Colours to soothe the mind during its gentle, yet relentless demise. Colours to ease the rage against the dying light.

'That told *me*,' she told the clock.

Gemma, of *all* people, had forced her to question her own attitude. Well, that would teach her to be such a smug, self-righteous little know-it-all. She'd been so busy considering Tom and Rosie's fabricated reality, their made-up facts, that she hadn't placed sufficient value on the *actual* truth. *And the truth will set you free*, said a little voice inside her head. A good man said that once, she thought.

'So what's the answer then?' she asked the clock.

Love is the answer, persisted the little voice.

'A quote by another good man,' conceded Chrissie.

The clock ticked its wholehearted agreement. And right there and then in that beige and cream room, four hours after the end of her shift, Chrissie had an epiphany.

Chapter Eleven

News of Rosie's condition is the worst kept secret in the neighbourhood and most of her friends and acquaintances have severed contact. But still, on the morning of her wedding to Tom, she sits on the swing under her beloved oak tree, feeling like the most fortunate girl in the world. She is keeping watch for her closest friend, Lillian, who has promised she will sneak over to wish her well and lend her "something borrowed". As Rosie moves gently to and fro, luxuriating in thoughts of her husband-to-be, she spies her old friend running down the sweeping driveway, dishevelled and lovely, red hair flowing behind her in a glistening stream. Lillian throws herself into Rosie's open arms and thrusts a small packet into her hand.

'It's a brooch,' she pants, 'a four-leaf clover. I hope it brings you luck, darling Rosie.'

Tears are streaming down her face.

'Don't cry for me, Lil. I've never been so happy.'

'I'm so sorry I can't be there to see you get married,' she sobs.

'You've done enough. Just being here now is enough.'

Lillian nods and pats Rosie's hand, gnawing nervously on her bottom lip.

'Mum would kill me if she knew I was here.'

Rosie laughs.

'There was a time when she was desperate for us to spend time together!'

Lillian blushes and smiles apologetically.

'Her Lillian. Rubbing shoulders with a politician's daughter.'
'Oh how the mighty have fallen,' says Rosie.

Rosie sat down heavily on her bed, staring at the old trinket in her hand. Lil's four-leaf clover brooch. The morning of her wedding to Tom… it all came flooding back to her. She looked around the room. She wanted to show Tom the brooch, the significance of which would surely not be lost on him. Where had he gotten to? Ah, she remembered now. He had come up to bed with her, but had then been whisked away by a large man wearing some sort of apron-like garment. They'd been terrified at first, but then she'd realised that the man meant them no harm. For some strange reason, which she couldn't quite make sense of, he lived with them in the house. She'd whispered to Tom to follow him and he'd gone off quietly enough. Afterwards, she'd taken down her smell collection and knick-knack box and tried to rummage and sniff away the pain. She'd found the brooch at the bottom of the box and felt a pang of guilt. It was supposed to have been "something borrowed", it had never meant to be for keeps. Dear Lillian. Rosie wondered where she was now.

Rosie's bedroom door flew open and in bounded Blondie, looking even more tousled and uncombed than usual.

'If you love him, then you should be with him!' she gasped. She leant against the wardrobe and took a few deep breaths.

'Eh?' The girl wasn't right in the head.

'I won't be here in the morning, but I needed to tell you that before I go.'

'Tell me what?'

The young woman placed her hands on Rosie's shoulders and scrutinised her weary face.

'You and Tom *belong* together.'

'Well I know that, you daft girl!'

Blondie chuckled and kissed her softly on the cheek.

'Be happy, Rosie.'

Their wedding is a simple affair, attended only by Tom's old mum and his adoring younger sister. Rosie's mother, who has orchestrated it all, cannot bring herself to be here and her father, who hasn't spoken to her since that awful evening, has sudden urgent government business to attend to. Rosie is sad that her parents' shame prevents them from sharing in her happiness, but has no other regrets. Not even when she stands in front of the grim-faced registrar, looking shyly down at her sensible navy blue skirt, with its hastily extended waistband, does she lament the lack of traditional ceremony. When the formal procedure is over, Tom turns to her and smiles.

'Hello wife,' he whispers.

'Hello husband,' she replies.

She is a wife! She is helped off the train by her new husband and stands proudly on the platform of Brighton station. She realises that her new social standing allows her the simple pleasure of holding Tom's hand in public and takes full advantage of this privilege now. Tom turns to her.

'Rosie…'

'Yes, my love?'

He lets go of her hand.

'I need to carry the suitcases.'

She laughs.

'Of course you do.'

He walks a few steps in front of her, but she doesn't mind. They are married. They are on their honeymoon. It is the happiest day of her life!

Tom awoke to find Rosie sitting on the end of his bed. He sat up and rubbed his eyes.

'Is it morning?' he asked.

She considered this. She'd been sitting on her bed for a very long time. She had watched the curtains turn from black, to pinkish grey. She'd listened to the fluting chorus of the pre-dawn blackbirds. Yes. Yes it was morning.

'Everything alright?' he asked.

'Do you remember our honeymoon in Brighton?'

'Can't say I do. Wasn't it Blackpool?'

'*Blackpool*?' she giggled. 'We've never been to Blackpool, you ninny.'

'Really? Only I'm sure we—'

'You always said you didn't like the sound of it. "Trashy" you said.'

'Did I?'

Tom shrugged and wriggled back down into his bed.

'Maybe you're thinking about Weston,' continued Rosie pensively, 'we went there once with Elizabeth. Just before the war broke out.'

'Elizabeth?'

'Yes. Don't you remember?'

He shook his head. Rosie was suddenly struck by a daring idea, equal to the many daring ideas of her youth, most of which had involved scrambling down the old oak after lights out, or smuggling Tom into her bedroom.

'Shall we go there now?' she suggested casually.

Tom sat up again.

'Weston?'

'Brighton.'

The more she thought about it, the more it made sense. They could *easily* get a taxi from South London to Brighton. Did they still live in Croydon? Yes, she was sure they did.

'We could have a sort of second honeymoon,' she continued, 'revisit all our old haunts.'

'I don't think I've ever been to Brighton,' mused Tom.

She laughed.

'Pack your bags. We're going on holiday.'

Gemma made herself a cup of tea and sat down to wait for the morning shift. It had been a difficult and upsetting night. Ellen had had another stroke and had passed away in her sleep. Gemma had been up and down the stairs dozens of times with paramedics and relatives, then there had been all the paperwork, cleaning and phone-calls. She'd almost lost her rag with Ellen's heartless younger son who'd actually had the *gall* to complain that she'd got him out of bed! Poor Ellen, thought Gemma. She'd been such a sweet old lady. Never any trouble and by far her favourite of all Greenacres' residents. Gemma stretched out on the sofa in the staff lounge and yawned. All she wanted to do now was to sink into a hot bubble bath and then get a few hours' kip. When her mobile phone began to ring, her heart sank. It was six in the morning. Only people ringing in sick rang at six in the morning. It was Mel.

'I'm still bad. Can you stay on until I can get another senior carer to cover?'

What could she say?

'Yeah, alright.'

The morning shift arrived and Gemma noted that Chrissie was late. True, she'd done overtime the previous day, but that had been her own choice, not agreed by management. She hoped the girl hadn't taken the morning off to make up for it. She'd be in serious trouble if that was the case. Another thought occurred to Gemma. Maybe Chrissie was too embarrassed to come in. Gemma felt a small stab of guilt for having so completely humiliated her the previous evening. After all, she thought, Chrissie was only a kid. Naïve and impressionable. She was at an age when she still believed in romance and love and this had affected her professional judgement. Well, it wasn't her problem. She always did her best to help and instruct the new recruits and she couldn't be blamed for their inevitable lack of experience. There was nothing for it now, she was going to have to call Mel and tell her of Chrissie's absence, but no point using up her own mobile credit. She let herself into the office and went to pick up the phone when something on the desk caught her eye. Two slim white envelopes, one addressed to her and one to Mel. She ripped open the one with her name on it.

Gemma,
Thank you for helping to open my eyes. You were wrong of course. Truth is not more important than love. In fact, love is

truth. Your lack of insight helped me realise that and I thank you most sincerely. You won't see me again, but I will always remember you fondly. Chrissie x

Gemma frowned. Was the crazy girl on drugs? She certainly looked the type. Well, whatever Chrissie's problem was, she'd obviously quit, so at least now she was out of her hair for good. Gemma allowed herself a smile before realising she was a member of staff down. She heard a shout from an upstairs bedroom. What the hell was wrong, *now*?! Two of the night staff scurried into the office, one ashen-faced, the other panting.

'Tom… Rosie…' wheezed the first.

'Gemma! You'd better get upstairs, quick!' rasped the other.

Gemma swore loudly and ran out into the hall.

'Thanks a bunch, Chrissie!' she muttered to herself, as she took the stairs two at a time.

Chapter Twelve

One beautiful morning in late spring, people strolling along Brighton's seafront were surprised to see a very elderly gentleman stepping shakily from a black cab, dressed in his Sunday best and carpet slippers. He was followed by a lady, who seemed just as old and frail, but whose eyes shone as brightly as the sparkling sea before her.

Tom shuffled slowly down the promenade. Watching his painful progress from the corner of her eye, Rosie was forced to acknowledge that he wasn't the man she'd married. She remembered the brisk pace he'd set the last time they'd come here together. She had hardly been able to keep up with him as he'd marched her around Brighton's tourist spots. In fact, she hadn't really enjoyed sightseeing with Tom on their last visit and, much as she was loath to admit it, she wasn't having much more fun this time. She stopped and turned to him.

'What's wrong?' she asked. 'Why are you walking so slowly?'

'I'm tired,' he replied, leaning heavily on his walking stick. 'Can we stop for a rest?'

She shrugged and headed for a nearby bench. Tom sat down with a loud groan.

'For goodness sake,' snapped Rosie.

Tom's eyes widened in surprise, but he didn't reply. Instead he took her hand and kissed it.

'I'm sorry,' he said.

'I'm sorry,' she whispers. It's their first ever quarrel and she realises too late that she has greatly angered him. 'I know you think I'm being awfully selfish, but I'm a wife and a mother now. I'm just thinking of you two.'

She strokes Elizabeth's soft downy head, hoping that she has said enough to placate him. He gives a harsh laugh.

'I'll tell you what. Let's telegram Chamberlain now and tell him Britain shouldn't go to war... because we've had a baby.'

She feels the tears well up behind her eyelids. She could never have imagined that her beloved Tom could make her feel so unhappy.

'I'm just saying it wouldn't be the best thing for our family.'

'Our family. Hah!'

She doesn't know what he means by this and is too afraid to ask. Afraid that the answer will bring her world crashing down around her ears.

'If war is declared, will you go?' she asks.

'Of course.'

She tries to gulp down a sob, but it escapes her quivering lips. He turns to her with a sigh.

'What would you have me do, Rosie?'

'Get a job here, in London.'

He shakes his head, incredulous.

'Where?'

'The Hoover factory. They're always looking for strong young men.'

She knows she is clutching at straws, that her suggestion is flippant and ridiculous, but she will say anything to keep him near her.

'Rosie!' he explodes. 'We're on the brink of war, for God's sake! Do you even know what that means?'

She nods, hiccups and bursts into tears. Elizabeth follows suit and soon mother and daughter are both wailing uncontrollably. Tom shakes his head, aghast.

'There, there,' he murmurs, patting his wife's arm.

'Tell me that you love me,' she weeps.

'I married you, didn't I?' he replies.

He makes her a cup of tea, the first he has ever made in their married life together, and waits for her tears to abate. She sips the overly-sweet liquid whilst soothing her still squalling child. When Elizabeth has been rocked, cuddled and cajoled back to sleep, Rosie takes her upstairs and puts her in the cradle. She comes back down to find Tom standing by the door in his shoes and overcoat. She knows better than to ask where he is going.

'We had fun in Brighton, didn't we?' she says, desperate to remind him of a happy shared memory. 'It was such a wonderful honeymoon.'

He kisses her lightly on the forehead.

'Yes dear,' he says, 'we'll always have Brighton.'

Brighton had changed a lot since her last visit. Rosie had never seen so many vibrant young people all in one place. Some of them were dressed very strangely; wedding veils and scanty frocks seemed to be the garments favoured by Brighton's youth. Even the men! The pier was the biggest shock though. The theatre that she and Tom visited on their honeymoon had disappeared and a big garish fun fair stood in its place. They bought ice-creams and found two deck chairs from which to watch the queer array of weird and wonderful passers-by. Rosie couldn't keep her eyes off the Ferris wheel. It was the hypnotic consistency which entranced her; round and round it went, a regular turning motion, which never sped up or slowed down. People got off, people got on and it repeated its monotonous cyclical journey. Tom nudged her.

'That looks like fun,' he smiled.

Rosie nodded, although really she thought it looked ghastly.

'I like it here,' said Tom, 'I don't think I've ever been before.'

'I wish you'd stop saying that,' she said, crossly. 'We came here for our honeymoon, I keep telling you.'

'*Did* we?'

'Yes. We came here, to this very pier and saw *Lady Windermere's Fan* at the theatre.'

Or was it *The Importance of Being Earnest*? She couldn't remember. But they had definitely seen something by Wilde. Or was it Coward?

'I don't see any theatre,' muttered Tom.

His furrowed brow filled her with anger.

'Why do you *always* have to contradict me?' she asked.

His eyes darted from side to side under her reproachful gaze.

'Where do you want to go now, sweetheart?' he asked eventually.

He looked up at her adoringly, which irritated her all the more. She felt cold and lonely all of a sudden.

'Come on,' she said, grimly, 'follow me.'

She knew exactly where she wanted to go. To the end of Brighton pier.

On the morning of Tom's departure, they awake in a clammy puddle of Rosie's perspiration. Elizabeth had demanded her attention most of the night, but the few hours she'd had in bed with him, she'd spent with both arms woven inextricably around his torso. Neither the uncomfortable heat of their eiderdown, nor his appeals for breathing space had made any difference; she would not let him go. The fear that had gripped her through the night now twists her bowels and forces her to spend half an hour in the outhouse.

'What a waste of our last few precious moments together,' she reprimands herself furiously as she checks and rechecks his bags.

Tom, by contrast, is quite cheerful and even whistles a jolly tune as he dresses.

'Chin up, darling,' he says, 'everyone says it'll be over by Christmas.'

But as he kisses her, with all the ferocity and exuberance of his youth, she knows somewhere deep within her churning gut that this is to be their final embrace.

They stood on the end of Brighton pier, shoulder to shoulder, eyes watering against the sea breeze. She turned to him, accusingly.

'Why did you leave me, Tom? I waited for you for so long.'

'I didn't, sweetheart. I *never*—'

'The baby was so young. You weren't even conscripted. *Why?*'

She prodded him angrily with a long crooked finger and he took a step back.

'I can't remember, I'm sorry.'

'You never really loved me did you?'

'I... I did, I *do...*'

'You only married me because I was in the family way.'

His face paled.

'*Please*. I, I don't know what you mean.'

She looked up sharply. She had never seen him looking so wretched and his rheumy eyes gave him the appearance of an old man. She buried her head in her hands.

'I sacrificed *everything* for you,' she wept, 'how could you abandon me like that?'

At once his arms were around her. He cradled her as the sobs she had pent up over a lifetime, racked her frail body.

'Hush, my darling,' he whispered into her hair, 'please don't cry.'

He lifted her face towards him and with his palms, smoothed away her tears. When he had finished, he led her to a bench, sat her down and covered her face, eyes and lips with the most exquisitely tender kisses she had ever known.

'Don't you know I love you?' he chided softly. 'Don't you feel it *here*?' He placed one hand over her, now mended, heart.

'Yes,' she replied simply.

He stood up and held out his hand to her.

'Come on,' he said, 'let's go home.'

About The Author

Tanya Bullock is a college lecturer, writer and award-winning filmmaker. She lives in the West Midlands with her husband and two young children. She has a passion for foreign culture and languages (inherited from her French mother) and, in her youth, travelled extensively throughout Australia, America, Asia and Europe. As a filmmaker, she has gained local recognition, including funding and regional television broadcast, through ITV's *First Cut* scheme; two nominations for a Royal Television Society Midlands Award, and, in 2010, a Royal Television Society Award in the category of best promotional film. In 2008, she directed a short drama, *Second Honeymoon*, which was screened at the Cannes Film Festival. On maternity leave in 2011 and in need of a creative outlet, Tanya began to write her first novel, *That Special Someone,* published in 2015. *That Special Someone* is a finalist in the 2016 People's Book Prize and The Beryl Bainbridge First Time Author Award.

http://tanyabullock.wordpress.com/
https://www.facebook.com/tanyabullockwriter
Twitter: @TanyaBullock15

Acknowledgements

Thank you to my husband, children, parents, brothers and their families. I love you all very much. An extra thank you to my talented husband, Darren Lewis, for another beautiful front cover.

Thank you to my friends and family who have supported me in my writing: Siobhan Aspley, Veronica Barnsley, Sarah Bent, Elizabeth Butters, Catherine Bullock, David Bullock, Keith Bullock, Marc Bullock, Matthew Bullock, Sarah Cassidy, Faye Cox, Bethan Crimmins, Catherine Davies, Rachel Davies, Susan Davies, Catherine Duckham, Becky Evans, Katie Fieldhouse, Claire Gibson, James Haigh, David Hastings, Maggie Hollowood, Gail Houghton, Ariane Jaksch, Jennie Jones, Ishani Kar-Purkayastha, Sarah Leonard, Matthew Lowther, Lauren Lenehan, Trudi Lenehan, Stephanie Lewis, Sarah Morgan, David Norchi, Kaush Patel, Sandra Peachey, Kelly Pearce, Lucy Perera, Nicky Pickles, Joanna Powell, Bev Roofe, Emma Speake, Angela Stocking, Jane Swanson, Joanne Taylor, Rowena Taylor-Oddoye, Louise Timms and Kelly Trobisch.

Thank you to Marge Brindley, Jodie Hewitt and the LRC team at Walsall College for bringing my work to new readers.

Thank you to the wonderful TS Harvey, a talented author and supportive friend.

Thank you to the charities, Kissing It Better and Soroptimist International: Stourbridge & District, for your support.

Thank you to Chris Harding and the rest of the wonderful
Walsall Waterstones team for championing local authors
(including me!).

Thank you to Rosalie Love at Blackbird Digital Books for your
invaluable help and advice. Thank you to my publisher, mentor
and friend, Stephanie Zia, for continuing to believe in me.

More Fiction by Tanya Bullock

That Special Someone (Blackbird 2015)

FINALIST for The People's Book Prize, The Beryl Bainbridge First Time Author Award, 2015/16

Life as the single mum of a learning-disabled teenager is tough. To Izzie's alarm, all her daughter Jaya, 18, wants from life is to get married and have babies. This creates a moral dilemma for Izzie. How she can continue to protect Jaya whilst at the same time letting her go?

"A wonderful story about the life, loves and struggles of a young woman with learning difficulties."
Jill Fraser
Director & Founder of KISSING IT BETTER
healthcare charity

ISBN: 9780993307003
Available as a paperback and ebook online and to order from all good bookshops, worldwide.

Keep up to date with all Tanya's news and new titles, join the
Tanya Bullock Mailing List
http://eepurl.com/O_cjj
(All email details are securely managed at Mailchimp.com and
are never, ever shared with third parties.)

If this book has lived up to your expectations, please would
you consider leaving a review? Amazon.com for US or
Amazon.co.uk for UK? A couple of lines is plenty. It really
makes all the difference to us small independent publishers who
rely on word of mouth to get our books known. Thank you!

Blackbird Digital Books
London

Discovering outstanding authors

http://blackbird-books.com
@blackbirdebooks

blackbird
77